Keeping Company

Keeping Company

GIBBONS RUARK

THE JOHNS HOPKINS UNIVERSITY PRESS
Baltimore and London

This book has been brought to publication
with the generous assistance of the G. Harry Pouder Fund
and the Albert Dowling Trust.

The Johns Hopkins University Press, Baltimore, Maryland 21218
The Johns Hopkins Press Ltd, London

Library of Congress Cataloging in Publication Data

Ruark, Gibbons.
  Keeping company.

  I. Title.
PS3568.U17K4   1983   811′.54   83-43
ISBN 0-8018-3041-9
ISBN 0-8018-3042-7 (pbk.)

for Kay

Contents

Acknowledgments

Grateful acknowledgments are made to the editors of the magazines in which the following poems (some in slightly different versions) first appeared:

Abatis: "Words Full of Wind from the Poulnabrone Dolmen"; *American Poetry Review:* "Essay on Solitude," "For a Suicide, a Little Early Morning Music," "Horse and Willow Tree in the Moonlight: Chinese, Sung Dynasty," "In the City without Wings," "Italian Bells"; *Bennington Review:* "Listening to Fats Waller in Late Light"; *Cumberland Poetry Review:* "Watching the Rain Shift at Flanagan's," "Words to Accompany a Small Bronze Horse from Orvieto"; *Graham House Review:* "Winter Love Poem to the Memory of Keats"; *Harvard Magazine:* "Autumn: An Empty Chair in the Tuileries," "For the Pause before We Decorate the Tree," "Sisley: Snow at Louveciennes, 1874," "Watching You Sleep under Monet's Water Lilies"; *Memphis State Review:* "Love Letter from Clarity at Chartres"; *Midwest Quarterly:* "Late Word from Corcomroe Abbey"; *New England Review:* "With Our Wives in Late October"; *New Republic:* "Lost Letter to James Wright, with Thanks for a Map of Fano"; *Ploughshares:* "To the Swallows of Viterbo," "Wildflowers Left to Live on Knocknarea," "Words to Accompany a Leaf from the Great Copper Beech at Coole"; *Poetry:* "The Goods She Can Carry: Canticle of Her Basket Made of Reeds"; *Poetry Northwest:* "Words to Accompany a Leaf from Sirmione"; *Raccoon:* "Thinking of Robert Francis at the Autumnal Equinox"; and *Swallow's Tale:* "Written in the Guest Book at Thoor Ballylee."

"To the Swans of Loch Muiri" and "Waiting for You with the Swallows" were first published by Friends of the Library, North Carolina Wesleyan College; "To the Nuthatches" was Palaemon Press Broadside #24.

Grateful thanks also to the National Endowment for the Arts and the Delaware State Arts Council for fellowships that supported the work on this book.

Keeping Company

Wildflowers Left to Live on Knocknarea

After a night of rain like a waterfall,
The stony lane that winds up Knocknarea
Is a runnel of swift water winding downward.
You should wear your Wellingtons and carry a stick.
The stones are slippery and the dog at the gate
Is fierce and requires a cheerful word in passing.

The way up is steep and then steeper and turns
On itself to give you again and again
The whole blue bay where it rummages the valley.
Nearing the top, the lane is nothing but a gully
Of wildflowers where you stretch for every foothold.
When, having stopped for breath, you can lift your eyes,

That stone shape just beginning to clear the high
Horizon is a queen's grave or nothing but stones.
Just over the final ridge, you can see it whole
At last, tired out and your breath entirely vanished,
So you simply sprawl out headlong in the heather
In an attitude a stranger might take for prayer.

But you are alone on the windy mountaintop.
North of that lighthouse are Rosses Point and the cliffs
Of Donegal. South and wild are the Mayo mountains.
If only the mist would lift you could see five counties,
But the low sky returns you to the near at hand.
There, nesting in the heather, you may uncover

The delicate wild blue harebell of Knocknarea.
If I know you, you will want to look at it long
And dream you can breathe the air it breathes forever,

Which is only to dream you can hold your breath forever
And not give in to the slow intake and exhalation
That keep you moving, even if your only way

Is the watery lane back down the mountainside.
The wind swings northward and cold. The mist is lifting.
It is high time you were picking your way downward.
Look for the blossoming ditch that brought you there.
Look. There is the spring gentian, there the small wild thyme.
Your turn has come to leave them there for another.

Watching You Sleep
under Monet's Water Lilies

B eloved, you are sleeping still,
Your light gown rumpled where it fell,

You are sleeping under the dark
Of a down comforter. The heart

Of dawn light blooming on the wall
Has not yet touched you where you still

Lie breathing, though it has wakened
The faint lilies, strewn and broken

Cloud-lights littering the water.
That you breathe is all that matters,

That you keep on breathing, lily,
While I wake to write this folly

Down, this breath of song that has your
Beauty lying among the pure

Lilies of the morning water,
Even though a light wind shatter

Them forever, and the too deep
Pool of desiring fill with sleep.

Essay on Solitude

During his pain, Rilke dreamed solitude
    An uncrumpled angel sleeping in the breast.
    Forgive me, companion lying fast beside me
In the light, breathing morning, I tell you he dreamed wrong.

    Human solitude is a slender single wing,
        The only thing born whole, undamaged, lovely,
        For all that flaring like a feathered wound.

        Though we move in an appreciation
    Of the sunlight, the sunlight will lengthen, stain,
    And blind stagger out, saying its name was morning.
Think of all the heart-dark solitaries we have known:

    Think of that dead cousin, lover of anything
        That worked, who oiled his rifle till the bullet
        Slept in the chamber, and then woke it up.

        His curled hair kissed his ear like a feather.
    Think of that live cousin, stunned by polio,
    Father and mother wreckage in the small-town bars,
Whose ruined legs flop above the foot-rests of the wheelchair

    He is dollying down the rampway to the school
        Ballet. His face is rapt at the clumsiest
        Of dancers, his gone legs wrapped in a rug.

        Think of how it took our handsome old friend
    All his life or merely one unbloodied hour
    To slow his breath to sleep, emptying the doorway
That he leaned and laughed in. Think of the summer running,

His running with it, edging the shallow surf-foam,
  Arms swinging loosely, shoulderblades surfacing,
    Flashing at us briefly, one at a time.

      What can we turn to from that sunburst back?
    Sunlight through the empty doorway glitters on
  The trefoil leaves of the green oxalis, the small
Wood sorrel I brought you on a whim a solid year

  Of our days ago, that still lives, that folds its leaves
    At the first sign of darkness, that opens them
      Secretly as eyelids at first dawning.

      We fall asleep dreaming of company.
    If we are not the perishing stars of flowers
  That come and go in a little cloud of leaves,
At least we are the leaves themselves, folding, unfolding

  Near our friends the others folded up forever.
    Each is one leaf hovering near another
      Dreaming two leaves can fly out of darkness.

      Leaves fall out of light. Each solitude owns
    A simple death shawl dreaming in some darkness
  Its raveled hemline grazes the earth like a wing.
It hurts to think between us we have a pair of them.

Late Word from Corcomroe Abbey

for Michael Heffernan

Brother, you were right: Even in the quick showers
Falling between brightnesses, this is an absorbing
Boneyard, every gone window, every fallen
Or half-fallen wall giving onto bay or Burren.
You were here in spring, when the briefest wildflowers
Lace the limestone crevices and try to repeat,
For all they are worth, the alchemy of late sunset

And the blues of water restless against the stones.
Now the hard hills are plainly the color of stone
And the light slips away by earliest evening.
Now, in the chill pause before the cold of winter,
I have come by Paddy Moylan's quiet directions
Up the road from Kinvara where he keeps his barroom
Friendly even to the likes of you and me.

I am sorry to tell you this, but Kennedy
Has gone from the mantel here and all over Ireland,
His brother having shoved his ghost off the deep end,
Disgraced himself and maybe destroyed a woman.
These people who spend their lives so near wild water
Have sufficient local drowning to suffer through.
So, on the wall is an empty square just the size

Of the map spread out between pints on the counter.
"Now," says Paddy, "you would be passing the Virgin
Who looks blindly out for the nine young ones dredged up
Body by body, scarcely recognizable
As creatures, days after the New Quay boat disaster.
She stands there blind as water in their remembrance.
Just beyond her is the road to Ballyvaughan,

But your way bears briefly away from the water
And into the farm lane climbing toward Corcomroe.
Remember to look for the tomb of Conor O'Brien."
On the north wall, near the derelict scars of some
Ancient painting, that King of Thomond lies stretched out
In effigy under a gable he would break
His head on if he ever attempted to stand.

A ripple of sun from one of the narrow windows
Crosses his hands where they lie crossed so on his chest.
If stone could pray, it would pray he died in his bed.
Too many have died out of bed on this island.
The light is going. Soon it will be nearly dusk,
When I will take the coast road back to Kinvara
And wait for the lovely old ones from Finavarra

To ease into Moylan's in their caps and kerchiefs
And bid me their deep and courteous good evening.
The quiet clock will be ticking, and after a while,
Though no one has spoken, we will idle over
To admire the simple painting of Corcomroe
Bestowed on Paddy when he laid down his books
For his barrels, schoolmaster to his village forty years.

They have thought to embrace him in more than his years,
To give him an abbey corresponding fondly
To the finer abbey elevated in his mind,
The windows emptied of all but his native view,
The water-smooth gravestones punctuating the gravel,
The unadorned, intricate, rain-bejewelled stonework
That keeps time here precisely to the century.

With Our Wives
in Late October

for James Wright

Wandering with weather down the long hillside,
We come to the slender reeds in the water,
All of us who lazed by our own rivers
    Summer and autumn,

Looking for redwings or leaves that were falling,
Light that was flying, the red wing of summer,
Never dreaming to be by one sure river
    Gathered together.

Now by the slender reeds in the water
Annie and Kay are looking for spiders,
Their own thoughts slender as the thoughts of spiders
    Looking for women.

Diligent spiders are our kindred creatures,
Friends of the season, and they are raveling
Somewhere lonelier than I can follow
    With all my singing,

But here's one Annie has suddenly sighted
Loitering brightly over the water,
Letting his legged and delicate star-body
    Flash us a signal

Clearer than water or the redwing's shoulder:
Some stars in heaven already dying
Light up the moonless night that is coming,
    Some stars are other

Bodies altogether, reluctant to say
How they become the light of October,
This spider, these leaves, these loveliest
     Faces of women.

Lost Letter to James Wright, with Thanks for a Map of Fano

Breathing his last music, Mozart is supposed
To have said something heartbreaking which escapes me
For the quick moment of your bending to a dime

Blinking up from York Avenue, the last chill evening
I ever saw you, laughter rising with the steam
From your scarred throat, long-remembering laughter,

"Well, the old *eye* is still some good, anyway."
I thought of your silent master Samuel Johnson
Folding the fingers of drowsing vagrant children

Secret as wings over the coppers he left in their palms
Against the London cold and tomorrow's hunger.
You could not eat, I think you could scarcely swallow,

And yet that afternoon of your sleep and waking
To speak with us, you read me a fugitive passage
From a book beside your chair, something I lose all track of

Now, in this dim hour, about the late driftwood letters
Of writers and how little they finally matter.
You wrote to me last from Sirmione (of all things,

Sirmione had turned gray that morning), and it mattered.
We were together when the gray December dusk
Came down on snapshots of the view from Sirmione,

Sunlight ghosting your beard on the beach at Fano.
I had thought to write you a letter from Fano,
A letter which could have taken years to reach you

On the slow river ways of the Italian mails,
And now I write before we even come to leave.
We are going to Fano, where we may unfold this map

At a strange street corner under a window box
Of thyme gone to flower, and catch our breath remembering
Mozart breathing his last music, managing

Somehow to say in time, "And now I must go,
When I have only just learned to live quietly."
Last time I saw you, walking a little westward

From tugboats in the harbor, your voice was already breaking,
You were speaking quietly but the one plume of your breath
Was clouding and drifting west and away from Fano

Toward the river ferry taking sounding after sounding.

Autumn: An Empty Chair in the Tuileries

My eyes keep wandering beyond this photograph
To another, where it is already winter,
Though in the branches of an earlier year.
A slow, affectionate walk up the Rue Mouffetard,
And now the clear blue light and a slender woman's
Accurate eye have found us standing together,
Hands in our pockets, bundled and bearded
Against the cold and suddenness of weather.
Just last night it snowed in the Tuileries,
Snow chastened the maws of lions, the little
Horses of the carousel had manes of snow.
Now, just over your head, the word *charcuterie*
Beckons you inward like an aromatic smile.

In this newer photo there is nobody,
Not even the little horses at a standstill.
In this one the leaves have only begun to fall.
Many of them are green, a few are barely bronze,
And the empty chair is so gracefully slender
Its shadow is lost in leaves and the bronze of sunlight.
The leaves will scatter soon, the cloudless sky
Will thicken with cloud and cold, and before I can
Notice and say so to a friend, the year's first snow
Will be falling again in the Tuileries.
In the poor light of a dream, my eyes keep on
Confusing one season with another,
Though even a dream should find no likeness there.

Words to Accompany
a Leaf from Sirmione

You were walking alone
Down the slender almost-
Island of Catullus,
Walking the one green lane

Toward Desenzano,
In your arms the warm bread,
Olives, and the cool heady
Wine of Bardolino.

You were troubling your calm
Head for the local name
Of whatever leaves came
Springing fragrant as balm

To burden your pathway.
You broke a sprig off, touched
Your face to it, then placed
It in your hair, the bay

Of Sirmione, laurel
You tossed me in our room,
Wondering what its name
Was in your casual

Headlong lovely hurry
To sunbathe by the spindly
Willow rippling the friendly
Sunlit water where we

Swam and lazed and forgot
The laurel in the taste
Of bread and olives, the last
Wine fragrant as our thought.

Not knowing I was only
Awaiting all my life,
You gave your one bay leaf
Away in Sirmione.

I hid it in my shade,
That slender book where late
This gesture of leaf-light
Touches your shoulder blade.

For the Pause before
We Decorate the Tree

Dark pine tree hung with fragrance,
Your branches are all lit
With spiderwebs, small vagrants
Carrying light from twig

To twig, themselves the darkest
Stars I ever gazed on,
Vacant shinings like the points
Of some ghost constellation,

Its destinations darkened
But its ways still showing
Frail and luminous, broken
Light-net in the needles.

Dark pine tree light with spiders,
Stand there all afternoon
Lifting those fragrant branches
We will soon weigh down.

Dark pine tree beautifully
Dying into daylight,
Remind me late or early
How the evening gathers

Weight and gathers stillness
Till I lie down with her
And begin to touch her
In those places farther

From me sometimes than the stars
Are far from spiders
In your branches, than the years
Have fallen from her face.

I will kiss the good grave hollow
Between her breasts, her thin
Inner wrist, the cool shallow
Cup above her collar-bone,

All these and more, till near dawn
Light along her left wrist
Is a thread trembling from one place
Kissed to another kissed.

Dark pine tree hung with fragrance,
Are these scattered kisses
I imprint her with dark stars
Or simple darknesses?

Love Letter from
Clarity in Chartres

In this late moment of the year's first morning,
The sudden January sky is blue
And cold as clarity in Chartres.

They have shepherded me down here,
Our two enduring friends,
From the City of the Memory of Light,

The last December lights of the city
Shrouded yesterday in bitter rain.
Now the cold sky comes to us in Chartres,

Cold sky we were lonely for in Paris,
The cold sky of a lonely mind
That might blaze suddenly, lit with love.

Now in this quick darkness of the great cathedral,
It is no wonder the centuries of stone
And shadow have no word for what is luminous,

Having uttered it, in the old poet's words,
Silently over all the years.
Now every arch is shocked with light around me,

And I am standing in the sunlight of those years.
Nothing but such clarity could say how clearly
You shine to me through the blue silks of distance,

Your rare and womanly friendliness,
Your lovely sanity, your eyes as clear
And delicate and less than everlasting

As this sudden January light.
I am walking alone behind these two
Particular friends along the narrow river

Echoing the willows and the spires
Of the cathedral so immense and intricate
In a clarity of blue and cold.

Here in Chartres, this solitary sun,
Radiant as it is, seems to be wandering
Longingly after its own peculiar genius,

Thinking maybe to go down once in its too long life
Behind a remarkable hill in America,
The western slope of your own left shoulder,

Happy to light just briefly before it darkens
Forever your long articulate back
Whose brave architecture dreams

It will never sleep.

Sisley: Snow at Louveciennes, 1874

She is rounding the corner by the garden gate,
Umbrella in her left hand, right hand casually
Warm in her pocket, as if she walked in sunlight

Deeper than the snow of sunlight in her memory,
Sunlight of that serious day in 1850,
Years ago, when he stopped by the wall and spoke her name.

She must have looked up from gathering in the garden
Sunlit grapes the color of cold leaves in the snow,
Maybe the color of the gate she does not enter,

The gate she left behind so strangely swinging open,
Encouraging the garden to riot in the street.
Not even the village sisters thought to murmur riot

When she left the village for a larger village
With her friend the stranger, for a few nights of closeness
And late wine and a few days of the clear river light,

Before he walked her home and left her in the garden.
Now the stone walls, chill and indifferent in the summer,
Are ruddy in the snowlight as the warm tomatoes

Abandoned to sunlight in her mother's basket.
This is Louveciennes. This is a once known woman
Rounding a corner the color of the gate

She does not enter. Snow is her memory of light.

Thinking of Robert Francis at the Autumnal Equinox

Clear everything out of your head but the sight
Of one man lifting his thoughtful head
To late September, in the early evening.
He moves so slowly you know he means to last.
He moves alone but his lamp may yet light
Faces of friends before the stars come clear.

Look where he moves at ease about the unclear
Boundaries of his summer garden site,
Look where he turns the sweetbriar to the light
And bends to gather the last fresh parsley hid
By fallen leaves. His watchfulness is a last
Signpost to turn his friends toward him and evening.

When they arrive sunlight and dark are evening
The odds against his cottage, whose clear
White walls and windows have withstood the last
Resorts of thirty winters. They know this sight
From other summers, and when he turns his head
And slowly as the late sun levels his light

Gaze to greet them, you are not surprised that light
Includes you in its welcome. The edge of evening
Is the flat stone lying like a little head-
Land at his single door. Then there is the clear
Wine of the dandelion, and the slow sight-
Reading of the gathered faces like a last

Uncertain harmony not meant to last.
He is naming over the birds that light
His windows in all weathers, naming the sight
Of the brash jay flashing his wings at the evening.
He is saying a poem for you in such clear
Tones, the sound alone illumines his head.

He is showing you a stone shaped like a head
And you are leaving, relishing the last
Wine on your tongue, entering again the clear
September weather where he shines his flash-light
Down the driveway to the road out of this evening
And stands there quietly watching you out of sight.

He waves you the last farewell of his evening,
Then sets his sights by star- instead of flash-light.
Thinking him gone, clear everything out of your head.

Italian Bells

1
Fiesole: San Francesco

From the two morning hilltops of Fiesole,
Monte Ceceri and San Francesco,
The bells and the birds are calling each other.
I lie awake so near your sleeping breasts
I do not know which hill to listen to.

2 *Florence: San Miniato*

At noon there is nothing but white light and black shadow,
The white light and black shadow of the pure façade of San Miniato,
The white sound and black silence of the big trembling bell
   of San Miniato,
And you and I together on the intimate public hill of San Miniato,
Shade and his sunlight, sunlight and her shade,
And nothing to do but mingle our hands above the river.

3
Fiesole: The Duomo

In the bluing dusk of the small piazza,
The old Italians know what time of day it is.
Already they are sipping darkness from their glasses.
A few feet nearer the stars, where we lie together
Wakeful under the high light of an open window,
We do not see the evening climbing from the valley.
It is true there are darknesses of air
In the tiny caves impossible to fill between our bodies,
But when the swinging bell floats up and tries to touch us,
Even the darkest interval is musical.

Winter Love Poem to the Memory of Keats

—the truth is there is something real in the World   Your third
Chamber of Life shall be a lucky and a gentle one—stored with
the wine of love—and the Bread of Friendship—Keats to Reynolds

1 *Assisi*

Here in Assisi, even the winter rainfall
Falls like a delicate shawl of benediction,
And the low westward sun so late coming out
Comes into our room and waits
Like a patient superfluous lover
For us to wake together and go out walking
Where the streets become the evening of light.

And you, Keats, how many times were you able even
To get out of bed and see from your Roman windows
The banked fire of azaleas on that stairway
Or the water flowering in Bernini's boat of stone?

Whenever I read you, you are older than I am.
Now you are younger than my younger brother,
And I have spent the afternoon in sleep
Or being wakened by the one breath's rise and fall,
And now the sunlight patient in the window
Calls our names and waits for us to follow.

There was one whose name you could not say in Italy
For fear your breath would fan those coals to flame
And burn away your breast to nothingness.
You could not bear to leave her.
You could bear to die.

What am I doing here with one whose name I say
In starlight and again in winter rainfall

And who answers where we walk together toward the evening
Of light?

It has happened before, the evening of light
Becomes the darkness and the darkness
Will become the morning
When we leave Assisi, feeling so good together
We believe no evil can befall us,
Even though we saw the great cross of Giotto
Flying above us in light and then in darkness,
Even though we saw on the bright post card
They have cut the weeping angel out of the picture.

2 *Rome*

Lusty club-footed Byron could have helped us maybe
When those thieves roared down like wolves upon us
On their Yamaha in Rome in early afternoon.
After all, he limped down out of his rooms
To lift a beaten stranger from the streets of Venice
While every good Italian darkened his window
And kept his counsel with the empty moon.

You would have been too weak where you lay just breathing.
Old poet younger than my younger brother,
You spent what was left of your generous heart on shipboard,
Nursing a poor consumptive girl in the racking waters
The way you nursed your brother in his storm-tossed bed.

Swift out of nowhere but the Roman sunlight
Came a kindly girl who knew those thugs
Had cleaned out all our cash and more of our Italian,
And she lifted that one whose name I say in Italy
Up from where they dragged her face-down down the stones
Before they vanished through the stalls of pears and artichokes
Into the suburbs scabbing the heart of Rome.

My love went out to have her coat sewn back together.
I went to read the letters in your room.

Words on your firewall were the only words I read:
"Sometimes, on this fireplace, Joseph Severn

Cooked meals for his friend John Keats."
I left you clearly where you are no longer,
Thinking to travel north toward Rilke
In his silence where he stayed along the Arno,
Wanting to live so quietly he would not surprise
The violets flowering by his rose-stone wall.

3 *Florence*

Today entirely in one sitting I killed a bottle
Of clear medicinal water in your name,
Then in it stood a rose with a three-foot stem
So she can watch it bloom beside her bed.

Last evening we were with the beautiful Sanis
For loaf after loaf of crusty bread and the earthy
Dark unearthly wine of the countryside,
And she told them how on autumn evenings in that year
I watched them out of my window,
Guido and Bruno, brotherly father and son,
Where the wood fire cached in the stone wall
Roasted the quails and lit their faces in the garden,
And two young birds who were always out after sunset
Came and lit on the back of Guido's chair.

She is sleeping now beside the only rose she owns.

Like you she cares not a straw for foreign flowers,
But in that spring she planted in a great stone urn
The delicate shining flames of red *impatis*,
Which burn alike in Rome and Hampstead and the Carolinas,
And left them for Marcella when we left for home.

She found in that spring lying beneath your stone
Fast-fading violets covering the earth that holds

Your bones were nearly hidden singing in their leaves.

Tomorrow I am flying with her to a country
Where an old man says you were a brave and noble maker,
Misburied by your bitter epitaph.

Did you see her, Keats, in the glazed momentary window
The spring rain made of your gravestone?

Words to Accompany a Small Bronze Horse from Orvieto

Now, in the late March light from our landscape
Where only the reeds and a few windy pine trees

Believe our human wandering above sea level,
The bronze mountain horse of Orvieto stands,

His slim right foreleg poised above our sideboard.
Horses like him fell asleep for centuries

When the great landslide of Etruscan darkness
Covered that ancient hillside like a solid ocean.

Last spring, before we mourned one friend of Italy
And horses in a cliff church lifting over the Hudson,

We passed the broken piecemeal horses shadowing
The way to where the one whole horse of San Marco

Rippled his bronze mane far from Venetian rain.
I kept returning to the ones not wholly there,

The Greek one little more than flying rear legs
And a tail, the Roman one they hauled up

Out of years of rubble in Trastevere,
His slim right foreleg missing, a rear leg missing,

Rider and saddle of the bare back torn away.
The sunlight cracked through nearly half his throat.

We left him to sing for a friend along the river.
Then we came to early summer and Orvieto,

Where we left our window open on the drowsy
Flies and the bells of the cooling evening,

Melodious clatter of stoneware when the lights
Blinked on in the alley's neighboring kitchens.

Most of the louder machinery fell asleep.
We walked hand in hand through the emptying streets

Downhill to where we caught the drift of music.
It was then the one horse shone in the window,

His foreleg lifted, his crimped mane following
The finely arched neck to his forehead, and then

He nearly shivered from dusk in his nostrils.
In the morning you awoke to find him with you.

You wrapped him in a blouse and carried him down
That hill and home to this room across the ocean.

He is still shining. The sideboard oak is shining.
Who knows if, gravely lowering his head to sniff

The bronze meadow of his own shadow, he may not
Still know a way to move from one home to another.

In the City
without Wings

Sometimes, in a hill town like Orvieto or Assisi, one can believe for whole moments in the possibility of a life with wings. Here, in this city of the river valley, stolid and beautiful as it is, no creature but a true bird could ever lift up of its own accord, circle once the bell tower of the Badia Fiorentina, where Dante used to look longingly at Beatrice during Mass, and fly away. Nonetheless, however much or little it matters, I am writing this in a small notebook covered with tentative brown wings, touched only slightly by a single feather of blue here and there, every one of them laid down by the hands of the printer Giulio Giannini. It is now late afternoon in Florence, and my head is full of wings.

Early this morning, after the market carts rattled noisily out of the doorways and into the streets below our window just about dawn, I lay awake at ease and watched her put her clothes on carefully and slowly, taking obvious pleasure as she grew warmer, her feet still bare on the chilly floor. I did not speak a word or make a move to touch her. Her hair is dark, her waist is slim, and she bends beautifully to whatever she wants in her luggage. Her neck is long and slender and made for adornment by the necklaces of Egyptian beauties, like those we saw yesterday in the Museo Archeologico.

We ate our small breakfast of rolls and coffee in the dining room directly outside our bedroom door, almost the only sound in the place the bickering of a pair of caged birds from an air shaft beyond the kitchen window, and then we went out to walk through the market. The only living wings we saw there were the pigeons whirring and coasting around the brutal statue of Cosimo on the corner in front of San Lorenzo. She leaned to drink from the fountain at his feet. She was holding a freshly peeled tangerine in her left hand.

Together we left the market and walked slowly together down toward the river. As we walked she divided the tangerine judiciously, giving each of us in turn a moist shining piece until the whole was gone. The day was clear and the air cold, but even winter sunlight can warm the south side of a building in Northern Italy, so we stopped to sit and read the papers before we even got down to the river. Two days ago, we learned, it had snowed in Miami. She was born in Florida, and she hates the cold, but today she felt like taking off her gloves and warming her hands with only the tea and the sunlight.

The river was green in the light and looked a little cleaner than the summer river. We walked along it for awhile and then crossed over Ponte Santa Trinita and began idly to window-gaze along Via San Jacopo, going upriver in the direction of a place we thought we might visit for lunch later on. It was not long before we came to a spot where we liked to look through between the buildings at the river. We had looked for a good while before coming aware of the handsome twisting sculpture partially blocking our view. It had never been there before. It looked from a distance like it might be Paolo and Francesca, and that is who it turned out to be. They were linked together painfully but they seemed somehow to be climbing up each other's bodies into the clear light over the river. Beneath their intertwining feet were the famous words:

Quel giorno piu non vi leggemmo avante

We walked over to the sculptor's window and saw, through our own reflections, a number of small fine sculptures in the same ragged style as the larger one, and in their center a pair of raised hands. At first I thought the right hand, or what looked to me like the right hand, held a baton, the hands looked so like a conductor's hands, but then I realized the hand was empty, and the hands no less a conductor's than I had thought. They were Toscanini's, or so I guessed from a smaller statue of the whole man. I stood in front of the window raising my own hands, trying to discover where the conductor was being seen from, feeling confused about the location of the thumbs, and then from out of the back shadows of the shop the sculptor himself appeared, walked over to the hands and smilingly and swiftly changed their positions so that they perfectly reflected my own tentative, exploratory gesture. Then he lifted his left hand, its fingers gathered to a point, briefly to his lips and then in our direction, as if to say "*Ecco!* If you want them to move, they move." I lifted my own hand in a grateful responding wave, and we walked away.

By this time the sun was well overhead and we stopped and ate a simple lunch at a place closer to the river than the one we had been looking for. Then we walked together back to our pensione, feeling warmed by the high sunlight, the wine we drank with our steaming pasta, and the rich small bronzes we had been lucky enough to discover. Back in our room we asked for some cold mineral water and after it was brought we closed the door and opened the tall window to sunlight angling across the bed. Then we undressed happily but without speaking and began each of us to read silently in whatever book came to hand. It was not long before the books by unspoken consent were dropped to the cool tile floor and lay there open face downward like a couple of dry leaves fallen from trees leaning later than they should be into winter, or two pairs of abandoned, sleeping wings. We had left behind the bronze articulate hands of Toscanini, and behind them the kissed, uplifted hand of the sculptor whose name we did not remember. We had given up even the faintest, most delicate thought of ever having wings, and our hands were everywhere.

To the Swallows
of Viterbo

You plummeting shards of the darkness,
You rising stars in the light still
Fumbling for the rickety trellis
Of morning, your suddenness fills

The whole unsteady air with whirring
Where we awaken quiet together,
Breathing soundlessly, no least stirring
While your wingbeats alter the weather

Of daylight arriving beyond
The window, quick-feathered rushing
And calling becoming a kind
Of rainfall in Viterbo, brushing

Us over with a mist so fine
The flawed hinges of our shoulders shine.

The Goods She Can Carry: Canticle of Her Basket Made of Reeds

Beginning I will praise a fine beginning,
How the cloud of sun came up over the marshland
Where the reeds were green and supple and wind-bent,
Not yet bent by the veiny hands of the craftsman
Who wove them in her basket while she watched and smiled.
Even the first time, coming home from the craftsman,
She brought me a round and steaming loaf of bread.
That loaf broken open on the kitchen table
Left loaves of sunlight piling in the empty basket.
One morning a week the blouses and the bedsheets,
The schoolgirl smocks and all the delicate underwear
She carries in the basket to the small Signora
And comes back grinning with an apple in each bare hand.
On an ordinary evening, maybe an evening
Enough like this one it could happen even now,
She comes with her basket of reeds overflowing
With basil and fennel, with sweet ham from Parma,
With fruits of the commune, with flowered zucchini,
With a slender green bottle of Veronese wine.
If I see her through the window I'll just
Whistle softly so she'll look up and right now she
Looks up and sees me and carries her goods up the stairs,
Calling "Buona sera" to the neighbors as she climbs.
Beautiful she brings the basket through the doorway
And pray do put it down I hear myself praying
And let it sit there while the evening sky turns starry.
In the evening, in the late weather of October,
The wine will cool on its own for a solid hour.
She slips her coat off as she turns to greet me.
Ending I praise her for putting the basket down.

Words to Accompany a Portrait from Verona

That afternoon in Verona
A fine rain blown downriver
Hurried us into a small courtyard,
Where we looked up to discover
A face disappearing quick
As a breath from the windowpane,

Ethereal, for all we know,
As this rare face so touched with light
By Pisanello, who forgot
Her name remembering her hair,
The breathing arch of her nostril,
Profile so lovely he was frightened

To think of her turning his way.
She was trembling when she left him,
Afraid of a father's anger,
And huddled her face in a cloak
Through the courtyard, down the alley,
In the back and out the great door

Of the church, her bared head chastened
And filial again, the look
That held the dazed Pisanello,
That holds us now, gone from her lips
Like jeweled moisture from the font.
Who were we for her to shy from,

Hurrying alone together,
Lovers welcoming slight shelter
Under a balcony of stone?
We looked up and she was gone.
In the hall she must have brushed through
A dark girl gave us this portrait

To memorize Verona by,
Brief hour of Verona, shimmering
Wet streets of a late afternoon
When disappearing rainfall left
Your face so frankly glistening
I thought to call it light.

Basil

There in Fiesole it was always fresh
In the laneway where the spry grandfather
Tipped you his smile in the earliest wash
Of sunlight, piling strawberries high and higher
In a fragile pyramid of edible air.
Light down the years, the same sun rinses your dark
Hair over and over with brightness where
You kneel to stir the earth among thyme and chard,
Rosemary and the gathering of mints,
The rough leaf picked for tea this summer noon,
The smooth one saved for *pesto* in the winter,
For the cold will come, though you turn to me soon,
Your eyes going serious green from hazel,
Your quick hand on my face the scent of basil.

Horse and Willow Tree in the Moonlight: Chinese, Sung Dynasty

for Joe Langland

The light I have here is the patient light
Of not long after sunrise, the window
That it shines through is the common window
Of a summer morning, the room is empty
Now of every wish but patience breathing.
The light and I are looking at the stillness
Of a field before the dawn in China,
The empty room as fragrant as the field.
I feel the light you may have felt, the air
I breathe is breath you may have taken on a
Tentative moonlit morning in the summer
Hills of Iowa, fifty years ago,
The cows still breathing darkness in the haybarn,
Father and mother still amazingly asleep,
Eight brothers and sisters all still sleeping,
Or maybe two or three have crept from the house
In their nightshirts, gone down to wake their still
Dreaming bodies in the cold dawn of Bear Creek,
Their pleasure to wash the sleep from their eyes
By entire immersion. They cannot know
You too are awake in the western pasture
Where the moon bathes the leaves of the willow
And the silvered horse you never dreamed is
Tethered, halter of worn rope around her head,
The frayed end knotted high among the branches.
A little moonlight sifts through the fabric
Of darkness, enough to whiten the fetlocks,
And it glows from behind her in a frail
Light line curving calmly from tail to mane.
Her white eye is the only eye you see,

The only light there is except for moonlight.
It would be easy enough to let her go,
But she is grazing in her own quiet light.
She does not seem to want to disappear.
Surely, watching her drop her wakeful face
To the grasses, you do not want her to.
You are still light enough to reach the high
Branches and loosen the rope for leeway.
Now you have climbed back down and walked away
And are standing still there as the moonlight
Watching her nuzzle the roots of the willow.

Working the Rain Shift at Flanagan's

for Ben Kiely

Whwn Dublin is a mist the quays are lost
To the river, even you could be lost,
A boy from Omagh after forty years
Sounding the Liberties dim as I was
When that grave policeman touching my elbow

Headed me toward this salutary glass.
The town is grim all right, but these premises
Have all the air of a blessed corner
West of the westernmost pub in Galway,
Where whatever the light tries daily to say

The faces argue with, believing rain.
Outside an acceptable rain is falling
Easy as you predicted it would fall,
Though all your Dublin savvy could not gauge
The moment the rain shift would begin to sing.

They are hoisting barrels out of the cellar
And clanging them into an open van,
Gamely ignoring as if no matter
Whatever is falling on their coats and caps,
Though the fat one singing tenor has shrugged

Almost invisibly and hailed his fellow
Underground: "A shower of rain up here,"
He says with the rain, "It'll bring up the grass."
Then, befriending a moan from the darkness,
"Easy there now, lie back down, why won't you,"

As if the man were stirring in his grave
And needed a word to level him again.
His baffled answer rising to the rainfall
Could have been laughter or tears or maybe
Some musical lie he was telling the rain.

This is a far corner from your beat these days,
But why not walk on over anyway
And settle in with me to watch the rain.
You can tell me a story if you feel
Like it, and then you can tell me another.

The rain in the door will fall so softly
It might be rising for all we can know
Where we sit inscribing its vague margin
With words, oddly at ease with our shadows
As if we had died and gone to Dublin.

Waiting for You
with the Swallows

I was waiting for you
Where the four lanes wander
Into a city street,
Listening to the freight
Train's whistle and thunder
Come racketing through,

And I saw beyond black
Empty branches the light
Turn swiftly to a flurry
Of wingbeats in a hurry
For nowhere but the flight
From steeple-top and back

To steeple-top again.
I thought of how the quick
Hair shadows your lit face
Till laughter in your voice
Awoke and brought me back
And you stepped from the train.

I was waiting for you
Not a little too long
To learn what swallows said
Darkening overhead:
When we had time, we sang.
After we sang, we flew.

Words Full of Wind from the Poulnabrone Dolmen

for Fred Chappell

So many random and accidental
Stones, you have to slow down even when walking
To watch the solemn deliberate rise
Of Poulnabrone: bare proscenium of stones
Ranked strangely to resemble the letter
Pi, clue to the circle's mystery upended
In a waste of limestone, though the schoolbooks
Tell us not even marauding Romans

Reached this island, much less the ciphering Greeks.
These stones remind me of a few old friends,
Or else those friends are steadying as stones
Reared upward on the wind-bitten Burren,
Bluff stones inviting the homesick traveler
To thread his way from light to empty light

Through the eye of a grave long washed away.
Were you to stand here weighing the options
You might decide to have a smoke instead,
Match after damp match failing till you turn
Your back on the dolmen, turn up your collar
And cup your face in your palms to windward,
Where, when you look up to study the distance,
You can just make out Kinvara in the snug

Of a sheltering cove, folding companionably
In on itself, though the gaps between houses,
Even narrow alleys blind to the bay,
Will let the weather through as light or wind
Or rainfall. The best stones there are novices
Compared to these, still dream of being hearths,

And one may now and then harbor a fire
For an hour, and a man may warm his back
Before it, lifting a glass and uttering
An odd welcome to a stranger, Latin
Or Gaelic, a scholar like you would know.
Just now I feel a native lonesomeness
In me say to hell with archaeology,
I must bestir myself on down the road

To where an old bartender, loneliness
Of Ireland on his tongue, marked up my map
Of County Clare with a generous hand
At the gas pump, leaning in his suit-coat
Under the hood of my battered Fiat,
Free hand lifted like a civil salute

To his brow, trying to find the oil-stick
In all that glare, and I swear I called you up
There hunkering over your minuscule
Script when I saw him, lenses suddenly
Blank gold coins in the rims of your glasses,
That kind of man, paying out steadily
That kind of attention, the late cold light
Level as wind off water in the eyes.

Words to Accompany a Leaf from the Great Copper Beech at Coole

Deep shade and the shades
Of the great surround me.
In the distance, the house
Is a ghost over grass.
You can see clear through it.

This tree is standing still,
Great names gnarling the bark
Like the names of lovers.
What were they but lovers
Of this shadowing tree?

Last evening at Kilkee
The whole sky was westward
Over the Atlantic,
No nightfall but nightfall,
Dark with the local drink.

Then, early this morning,
A small mist followed me
Halfway to this garden
Along the Galway road
And then gave way to light.

What are we but lovers,
The one web of our lives
Veined nearly visible
Over the Atlantic
As this leaf shot with light

Though its veins are darkness?
Your face is before me,
Your green eyes shot with light.
What are we as lovers
But the one leaf only?

This tree will bear others.

For a Suicide,
a Little Early Morning Music

Most of the mornings here, when we awaken,
She and I can see what's left of the stars together,
And so we can this morning, even though lonely,

Imagining you. You were alight with elegance,
You were nervously and splendidly intelligent,
You loved the cities and you loved the shores,

You wanted to awaken with somebody.
Now, in this early morning, gathering
The last star's sunlight in a large warm bed,

We can see it clearly rising, rippling
A few temporary clouds with color
Over the water, and in the carved surf

A man of sixty, lean beneath his years,
Is swimming closely with a slender woman.
They must have awakened early together,

And then they thought of something they could do.
Sunlit in a place you loved, I can see you
Sunlit in another, you and I together

Down to our shirtsleeves in the brilliant streets,
Our neckties riffling as we round the corners
To Hester Street for veal and some wine from Verona,

Mulberry Street for pasta to carry home.
We were late for the train, and you were happy,
For you liked nothing better than wearing

A light suit, walking the streets in a hurry,
Packages under your arm for somebody lovely.
In Florence once, we saw the dark cool David

Of Verrocchio, and did not have the wit
To think of you running bareback through the summer.
From Rome we sent you a picture of Augustus

Looking under thirty in extreme old age,
But what we looked at longest was the beautiful
Bronze boy patiently and tenderly pulling

A thorn from his foot for several thousand years.

Listening to Fats Waller
in Late Light

for Tom Molyneux, 1943-1977

Once, in a Village bar, you kept us listening
To this music till we nearly missed our train,
Then hailed a taxi half-way to the station,
Your bright tie flying behind you like a little wake.
Now we are listening into late mountain light.

A little jazz in the South of France, Vence
Maybe, or some other town in the South
Of the heart, was what you dreamed you longed for.
Wine and daylight, the company of women
And children, the slow gold raveling of an afternoon.

The year we were for Italy, you were for France,
Their local wines so distant, yet the two countries
Closer in the end than our South and your North.
You were meant to visit us in Italy,
But your lame Peugeot would never make the hills.

Back home in the coldest winter yet, you nursed
Your broad-beamed Oldsmobile like a mother
With a sick child, bundling the engine at night
With old blankets, cajoling it to hold on.
Loaded with wine, it broke down on a Maryland road.

This is America. If this were in Europe
We'd send it to you on a sunny post card,
The lake water rubbing the stones with water-lights,
The small birches lonely even in their groves.
We came from your death to this beautiful place.

The sun goes down. He's doing "Honeysuckle Rose."
Were you speaking you would no doubt tell us

There is no clean way to come to this music
Save the one long mountain road of our grief.
There is no clean way to come to this place

Save the one long mountain road dead-ending
At the landing and nothing but the sunstruck lake.
This place appeals to your love of the sunlight
As our love for you appeals to the blue
Provençal light of your early absence.

For us the North Italian, for you the Provençal,
Those two skies nearer the one color than we thought.
Now the late light shines on our luck in each other,
A wish flashed over your shoulder as you left the party.
We are cooking the small-mouth bass and listening

To Waller, drinking the white wine of Verona
Since lately we get no kick from champagne.
Lucky the woman, lucky the man, relishing
Fresh dill, a little lemon and a little butter,
A little traveling music, a particular voice

Suddenly from no place at all in particular
Wishing us to live and be happy, have fun
Somehow tapdancing barefoot on the warm floor
Going cooler as the mountain sun goes down,
And the man himself, old friend, the man is doing

"Ain't Misbehavin'." We are getting mature.

Written in the Guest Book at Thoor Ballylee

This room needs furniture and the blue walls are cold.
Whether we should have been welcomed by the old ghost
We admire seems hardly civil to ask in County
Galway, where doors swing open to the rankest stranger
And they say whatever warms you when you are cold.
Still, this room needs furniture and the walls are cold
And colder in the resolute Atlantic wind.

This room needs music. I call old Tommy Nolan
Down from the streets of Galway with his great fiddle
And his frightening cough, to haul his chair up
Close to the measly fire we would be grateful for,
And lean into music. I call on Tony Small,
Laughing at the counter there in Cullen's, marvelous
Raw voice sweet with whiskey, to put down his glass and sing.

This room needs music and nobody here can sing.
Wind bangs the shutter. Long absences drum at the door.
Some voices we would gather the wind has scattered
All over this and other islands, some few as far
As the man who found and imagined this place, and then
Abandoned his soul to its battlements to die
In a French room without benefit of Galway.

We saw where they plowed him into that rainy churchyard.
He might have called his own bedroom the stranger's room.
Instead he chose this room where we stand wondering
How cold a man would call a room for guests the stranger's
Room, or how honest. Speech is exhaled into the cold,
Whatever we say, though rhetoric may turn to rain
And leave a lover's indiscretion in the air:

If you want to believe our life is possible, come
Look out the window where the wind blows a brief shower
Of leaves on the stream, swift with earlier rainfall,
And try to imagine that they love their vanishing
Merely to leave the surface untroubled and clear.
Then listen for breath in this room without music.
While you can hear it the stream makes a personal sound.

To the Nuthatches

Stubby stoneware
Nestling, thumb of
Brightness, you were
Shaped under hands

Steady as rain
Over Cornwall
Where you came from
Cool to her hand.

You, memory's
Brave suddenness,
Flickering blue
Wings in the snow,

You quicken her
To vigilance
At the window
Of a stone wall

Windows ago.
Small as juncos,
Slate-blue, breasted
White underneath,

You are her birds:
Little one nudged
Into a stone,
Wingflasher blue

As memory,
And you, last one,
Unseen nuthatch
Lit with desire,

Downward climber
Headlong for dark
Earth, breast astir
With all you have

Left to tell her.

To the Swans
of Loch Muiri

How she will love to see you here, you there,
Admiring yourself as if you were not
Simply one in a breathtaking hundred
Troubling this water to mirror your wings.
There is only the thinnest ridge of earth
Between you and that peerless shipwrecker,
Galway Bay, and yet you can coast serenely
As if you fell from the trees of autumn
To drift the surface of an inland pool.
You there, climbing thin air above the cloud
Of your reflection with a quick backward
Shudder and flourishing of your raised wings,
You are not the only beautiful one.
I am here to tell you just about now
There are great wings tilting in the airways
Over Jamaica Bay, outbound for Ireland.
Someone is leaning back becalmed as one of you.
She is flying in her sleep toward morning.
Now the earliest lamp of evening fills
A window set between us and the West.
The bluffs at my back have begun to darken.
One more midnight to live through, then to rise
Well before dawn and drive toward Kilcolgan
For the straight road south, the early morning
Dark a rush of roadside hedge at the window,
The right way dark as the bottom of some bay,
The only stars the lights of Galway City
And somewhere the vanished whites of your wings.
Keep them to my left and I will find her.
Right now our sky is turning toward that shade
I will wake in, a few of you are stirring

As if you had somewhere to go, singly
Or in the bowing couples beginning
To form and float together, and I feel
Already like that one of you I love most,
Wings whirring, long neck arched in expectation,
Half flying and half staying in the water.

B*orn in North Carolina in 1941, Gibbons Ruark
holds degrees from the Universities of North Carolina
and Massachusetts, and now teaches English at the
University of Delaware. His poems have appeared in a
variety of magazines, including* The New Yorker,
New Republic, Poetry, *and* American Poetry
Review, *as well as in anthologies and textbooks, including X. J. Kennedy's* Introduction to Poetry. *In
1979 he was awarded a fellowship by the National
Endowment for the Arts. His two earlier books of poetry are* Reeds *and* A Program for Survival.

The Johns Hopkins University Press
KEEPING COMPANY

This book was composed in Baskerville text and display
type by David Lorton, from a design by Susan P. Fillion.
It was printed and bound by the Maple Press Company.